D0580071

A Cool Summer Tail

by Carrie A. Pearson

Illustrated by Christina Wald

How do humans stay cool in the summer, Mama?
Do they hang out their tongues,
like a spring that's been sprung,
breathing fast in and out like this?

No panting! No puffing!
No *huh, huh, huh huffing*!
They sweat through their skin when it's hot.

How do humans stay cool in the summer?
Do they slide into ponds
under awnings of fronds
and let cool water wrap their shells?

No splashing with sunfish.
No stepping in mud-squish.
They swim in clear water with kids.

How do humans stay cool in the summer, Mama?
Do they perch in the shade
under leaves dappled jade
with their feet curling 'round a branch?

No perching on branches,
up high taking chances.
It's safer for them on the earth.

How do humans stay cool in the summer, Mama?
Do they lie bottoms up,
like a big furry pup,
spreading out on the cooler ground?

No napping on patches
of cool earth that scratches.
Their beds are much softer than ours.

How do humans stay cool in the summer, Mama?
Do they grow hair that's new
with a light, reddish hue
and with space in between for air?

No growing new hair—
the hair that they wear
won't change when the weather turns hot.

How do humans stay cool in the summer?
Do they hang from their hive
so their Queen will survive
using bee wings to blow in cool air?

No strong wings for chilling.
They wouldn't "bee" willing
to hang from a hive with their toes.

How do humans stay cool in the summer, Mama?
Does their tongue give a lick
on their arms as a trick
to make heat from their skin disappear?

No spit baths in summer.
They'd think it's a bummer
to use their wet tongue to keep cool.

How do humans stay cool in the summer?
Do they flatten their wings
shielding out what sun brings
so their bellies don't get too hot?

No wings as a shelter
so insides don't swelter.
Their bellies hang out in the sun.

How do humans stay cool in the summer?
Do they come out at night,
when the sun's lost its bite,
to eat food hiding under a log?

No shunning the sun beams.
No hungry for lunch dreams.
They munch on their food when they choose.

How do humans stay cool in the summer?
Do they dig in the dirt
so the sun doesn't hurt
their skin when it shines from above?

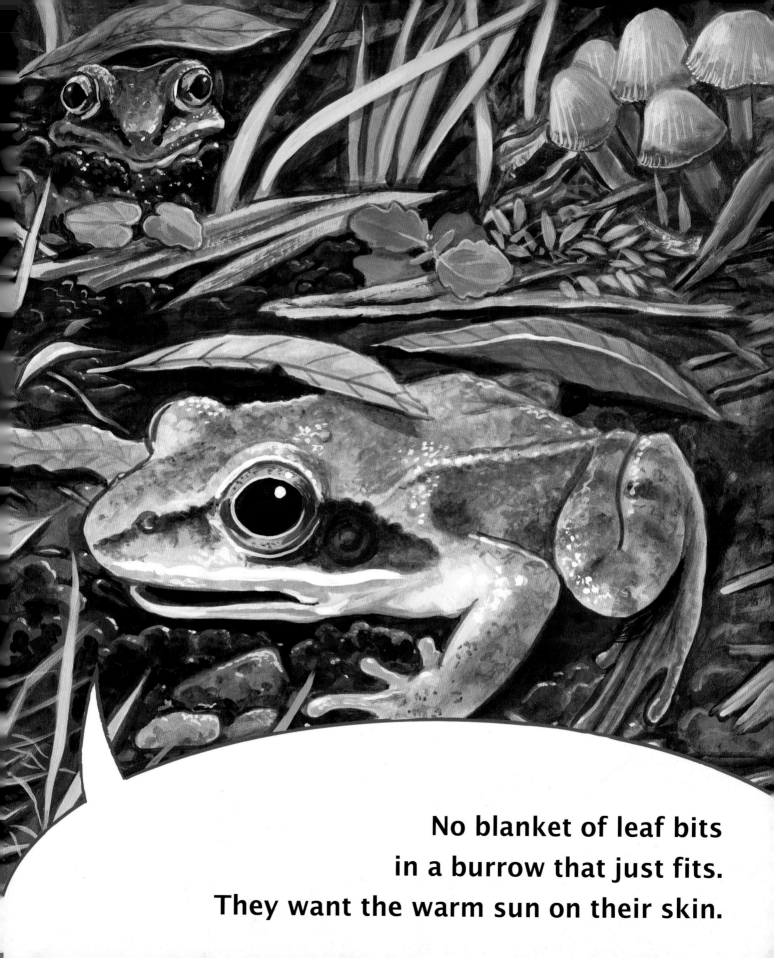

No blanket of leaf bits
in a burrow that just fits.
They want the warm sun on their skin.

How do humans stay cool in the summer, Mama?
Do they fly from the heat
traveling high with each beat
of their wings to a cooler home?

No leaving their nest site
in search of cool daylight.
They want the hot summer to come!

How do animals stay cool in the summer, Mama?
Do they trade in their clothes,
maybe show off their toes,
and then splash in a blue green pool?

No swimsuits, no flip-flops,
short shorts, or tank tops.
Their bodies know how to stay cool.

For Creative Minds

Animals and Summer Adaptation Fun Facts

Animals have many different ways to stay cool when summer temperatures soar. Which of these might YOU do to stay cool in the summer heat? Have you ever seen an animal do any of these?

Some mammals pant, or breathe in and out very quickly with their tongues sticking out. The moisture on their tongues cools the air going into their bodies, helping them to cool down.

All kinds of animals jump into or spray themselves with water or mud to cool down. The cooler temperature of the water or mud helps to cool off their bodies.

Some animals release water onto their outer skin (sweat). The evaporating water then cools the animals' bodies. Other animals don't make their own water or sweat so they have to put water onto their skin by licking themselves (spit bath).

Other animals might burrow into cool soil or hide under rocks. The cooler dirt helps to lower body temperatures.

Some animals hide in the shade where it is cooler.

Some animals migrate to higher elevations or cooler climates.

Still other animals might sleep or nap during the day and be more active in the evening or at night when it is cooler.

Summer and Winter Adaptations: Compare and Contrast

These animals are also featured in the companion book, *A Warm Winter Tail*. By looking at the images below, can you describe:

· How do the animals look the same or different in the summer and the winter?
· After reading both books, can you describe some of the differences that we might not be able to see?
· How does the surrounding area (the habitat) look? Is it the same or different in the summer and the winter?
· What are some things that might be different between the two seasons that you don't see in the illustrations but might be able to feel?

Summer Animal Matching Activity

painted turtles

grey squirrels

black bears

white-tailed deer

honeybees

black-capped chickadees

Match the animal to its description. Then match the colors to identify the animal classes. Which animals are insects, amphibians, reptiles, birds, or mammals?

1 These mammals don't have sweat glands like humans so they lick their forearms where their hair is thinner. The saliva evaporates and carries heat away from their body.

2 On a hot day, these mammals often lie on their backs, exposing their bellies with thinner fur. Their body heat escapes.

3 To lower their temperature, these cold-blooded reptiles look for the cool water found in ponds, lakes, and streams.

4 You can find these tough, little birds hiding from the hot sun under the shade of leafy trees. They also might stand with their feet in puddles of water, or open their beaks and breathe quickly.

5 In late spring, these mammals shed their heavy winter hair and grow a new coat of fine, short, reddish hair. This special coat allows air to move over the animals' bodies.

6 During the day, these insects fan their queen to cool her. At night, they may hang from the outside of the hive to catch the cooler air and fan it inside the hive.

Answers: 1) grey squirrels, 2) black bears, 3) painted turtles, 4) Black-capped chickadees, 5) white-tailed deer, 6) honeybees
mammals: grey squirrels, black bears, white-tailed deer
reptile: painted turtles
bird: Black-capped chickadees
insect: honeybees

black swallowtails

garter snakes

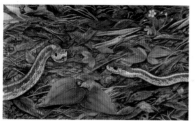

humans

Costa's hummingbirds

wood frogs

red foxes

7 These reptiles are good at keeping their temperature just right, but if it gets too hot, they might den up during the heat of the day and come out at night to eat when it is cooler.

8 When the weather is hot, these mammals turn on fans or air conditioning in their homes; wear light weight clothing; go swimming in cool lakes, rivers, ponds, or pools; and sweat to cool their skin.

9 These insects use the warmth of the sun to keep their bodies the right temperature. If they get too hot, their outstretched wings can be used as umbrellas to shade their abdomens.

10 To cool off, these mammals rapidly breathe air in and out of their open mouths and across their damp tongues (pant). The heat from their body evaporates with each breath.

11 Although these birds are tiny, they are able to fly great distances to cooler weather. They fly from the Southwestern Desert to the Pacific Coast in search of cooler temperatures.

12 These amphibians must keep their skin moist, even when it is hot and dry outside. So they dig under leaves and sticks to rest where it is cool and damp.

Answers: 7) garter snakes, 8) humans, 9) black swallowtail, 10) red foxes, 11) Costa's hummingbirds, 12) wood frogs
mammals: humans, red foxes
reptiles: garter snakes
birds: Costa's hummingbirds
insect: black swallowtail
amphibian: wood frogs

To Bonnie and Neil who have always helped me chase my dreams—C.A.P.
For the Cincinnati Zoo, one of my favorite sketching spots and to the painted turtles floating in the flamingo section that patiently let me draw them—C.W.

Thanks to Leslie Science and Nature Center (Ann Arbor, MI) staff: Pattie Postel, David Clipner, and Michelle Mirowski for reviewing the accuracy of the information in this book.

Library of Congress Cataloging-in-Publication Data

Pearson, Carrie A., 1962-
    A cool summer tail / by Carrie Pearson ; illustrated by Christina Wald.
        pages cm
    ISBN 978-1-62855-205-8 (English hardcover) -- ISBN 978-1-62855-214-0 (English pbk.) -- ISBN978-1-62 855-232-4 (English downloadable ebook) -- ISBN 978-1-62855-250-8 (English interactive ebook)
    1. Animals--Summering--Juvenile literature. 2. Heat adaptation--Juvenile literature. I. Wald, Christina, illustrator. II. Title.
    QL753.P425 2014
    571.7'6--dc23

                5497 0487 11/14

                        2013036387

Lexile® Level: 700

Key Phrases for Educators: adaptations, anthropomorphic, compare/contrast, repeated lines, seasons (summer)

Text Copyright 2014 © by Carrie A. Pearson
Illustration Copyright 2014 © by Christina Wald

Manufactured in China, December, 2013
This product conforms to CPSIA 2008
First Printing

Sylvan Dell Publishing
Mt. Pleasant, SC 29464
www.SylvanDellPublishing.com